This book belongs to:

. . . .

. . . .

Editor: Carly Madden

Designer: Hannah Mason

Series Designer: Victoria Kimonidou

Editorial Director: Victoria Garrard

Art Director: Laura Roberts-Jensen

First published in the United States by QEB Publishing, Inc.

3 Wrigley, Suite A, Irvine, CA 92618

www.qed-publishing.co.uk

A CIP record for this book is available from the Library of Congress.

ISBN 978 1 60992 808 7

Printed in China

Stinky Jack and the Beanstalk

Written by Steve Smallman

Illustrated by Neil Price

Once upon a time there was a poor young boy called Jack.

He lived with his mom in a ramshackle house in the country.

Jack was so lazy he couldn't
be bothered to wash himself.

He began to **smell so bad** that his
mom made him sleep in the cowshed!

Daisy the cow
was not impressed.

One day, Jack's mom said,

"We've got no money left!
Go and sell Daisy and
make sure you get a
good price for her."

But Jack sold the cow
for just a handful of beans.

His mom was so angry that she
threw them out of the window.

Overnight, the beans grew into a huge beanstalk!

The next day, Mom sent Jack up the beanstalk to pick some beans.

Jack climbed higher and higher, until he came to . . .

...a **giant's** castle!

Jack was hungry,
so he knocked on the door
and asked a kind-looking
lady for some food.

She let Jack in and gave
him a slice of sausage.

But then . . .

BOOM,
BOOM,
BOOM!

Huge footsteps were
heading their way!

"Hide before my husband comes!"
said the lady.

So Jack climbed into
an empty teapot!

"Nonsense!"
said his wife.
"I can't smell anything.
Eat your sausages!"

After lunch the giant started
counting his money.

Jack had never seen so many gold coins.

Soon the giant fell asleep.

Jack crept out and picked up a
gold coin that had fallen on the floor.

He hurried back down the beanstalk
and gave it to his mom.

"Good boy," she gasped.
"This will pay to fix
our house."

"Now, please, Jack,
take a bath!"

But Jack dashed back up the beanstalk.

Back at the castle, the giant's wife
let Jack back in. But then . . .

"FEE, FIE, FO, FUM!

I SMELL THE STINK OF AN ENGLISHMAN.

BE HE ALIVE OR BE HE DEAD,

I WISH HE WAS SOMEWHERE ELSE
INSTEAD!"
roared the giant.

"Nonsense," said his wife.
"It must be a clogged drain.
Now, eat your sausages."

After supper, the giant fetched a little goose and placed it on the table.

"Lay, goose, lay!" he cried.

Honk, plop, thud!
The goose laid a solid gold egg!

The giant soon fell asleep.

Jack quickly stole the golden egg and climbed back down the beanstalk.

Jack used the egg to buy back Daisy the cow.

But he still wouldn't take a bath!

"You're not coming into my new house until you're clean!" said Jack's mom.

Daisy wouldn't let him in the cowshed either!

So Jack had to sleep outside on a pile of leaves.

The next day, stiff and achy, Jack climbed back up the beanstalk.

Jack had just sneaked back into the castle when . . .

"**FEE, FIE, FO, FUM!**
I SMELL THE **STINK** OF AN ENGLISHMAN.

BE HE **ALIVE** OR BE HE **DEAD**,

I WISH HE WAS SOMEWHERE ELSE **INSTEAD!**"
roared the giant.

"Nonsense, my dear," said his wife. "Perhaps you've stepped in something! Now, eat your sausages."

That evening, the giant fell asleep
listening to a magical, singing harp.

When Jack jumped out of his hiding
place the harp shouted,

"YUCK, WHAT A STINK!"
and woke up the giant!

The giant grabbed Jack
in his huge hairy fist.

"Please don't eat me!"
cried Jack.

"I don't want to eat you!"
gasped the giant.

"I like having
visitors but only
ones who don't stink!

TAKE A BATH . . .
NOW!"

Jack ran to the bathroom.

The giant's wife
filled a tub with hot,
soapy water and at last,
Jack took a bath!
He even washed his hair.

He felt wonderful . . .
and he smelled even better.

Jack enjoyed himself and decided
that washing was fun!

The giant invited Jack to stay for supper.

"I'm sorry
I took your gold,"
said Jack.
"I gave it to my mom to fix our
house and buy back our cow."

"That's OK,"
said the giant kindly.
"Now, eat your sausage!"

"Do you have sausages
for every meal?" asked Jack.

"Yes,"
sighed the giant.
"I'd give a big bag
of gold for some
fresh vegetables!"

"Really?"
said Jack.

"Um . . . do you like beans?"